Clara Belle

Queen Bees and Wannabees: Outsmarting the School's Royalty

Queen Bees and Wannabees: Outsmarting the School's Royalty

by

Clara Belle

Prologue

In Jefferson High's ever-shifting labyrinth, the walls whisper secrets, and the lockers hold more than just books—they are archives of whispered rumors and silent battles fought in the shadows of adolescence. In this maze of youthful dreams and fears, Ellie found her calling, not as a warrior but as a witness.

With her camera as her shield and her keen eye as her guide, Ellie sought to capture the essence of those deemed untouchable—the queens of the social hierarchy whose crowns were made of glares and whispers. From the Cheerleader with her megawatt smile that could chill the air, to the Study Group Czar, whose intellect was as sharp as her patience was short, these girls ruled the corridors of Jefferson High with an iron fist.

But beneath the surface of their perfectly curated exteriors lay stories untold—of vulnerability, fear, and the deep desire to be understood. As Ellie peered through her lens, she saw past the armor of popularity and the weapons of wit. What started as a simple project to fill the yearbook pages became a journey into the heart of adolescence—a quest to transform the narrative from division to unity.

It was in the whispered confessions, the candid laughter, and the silent tears that Ellie discovered the truth: every queen bee yearned to be more than just a ruler of the hive. They were daughters, dreamers, and, most of all, survivors of the very tales they spun.

As the year unfolded, each click of the shutter captured more than just a moment; it captured a possibility—the chance to tell a new story, shed the old skins of labels and lies, and perhaps weave a tapestry of understanding that could clothe them all in dignity.

And so, beneath the flickering fluorescents and amid the echoes of locker slams, a transformation began. Not just of the queens but of the kingdom itself, driven by the quiet power of a girl who believed that everyone— no matter how high their throne— had a story worth telling.

Dedication

This book is dedicated to the silent observers and the unsung heroes. Such heroes watch from the edges, whose stories seldom make the headlines but whose hearts hold the deeper truths of our time. To those who believe in the power of empathy and the transformative light of understanding, may you always find the courage to tell your story.

Table of Contents

Clara Belle

Navigating the Hive

Queen Bees and Wannabees: Outsmarting the School's Royalty

Clara Belle

In the bustling halls of Jefferson High, a kingdom of sorts thrives amidst lockers and lined notebooks. Every student holds a place here, yet some wield their power from thrones built on whispers and glares. Among them, the 'royalty'—a group of girls known as much for their charm as for their ruthlessness—reign supreme.

Enter our protagonist, Ellie—a girl more comfortable in the shadow of a bookshelf than under the spotlight of high school drama. With her quiet demeanor and keen observational skills, Ellie often feels like an outsider, watching the intricate dance of social dynamics from the sidelines. Yet, it is this perspective that gives her an unparalleled view into the lives of the mean girls who set the tempo for the school's social scene.

The challenge of navigating a world ruled by these queen bees is daunting. They are not merely bullies but architects of insecurity, experts in exclusion. But beneath their polished veneer lie fears and vulnerabilities that drive their need for control. This book promises a deep dive into the world of these complex characters—dissecting their motives, unveiling their strategies, and, most importantly, offering a guide to outsmarting them.

"Queen Bees and Wannabees" isn't just a survival manual. It's a beacon of humor and empowerment—a testament that understanding your adversaries is the first step to overcoming them. Through detailed profiles, hilarious misadventures, and practical advice, we will navigate the social labyrinth together.

So, dear reader, prepare to arm yourself with knowledge and wit. Let's decode the secrets of surviving and thriving among the school's royalty. And remember, in the hive of high school, sometimes the quiet observer holds the power to become the queen slayer.

Clara Belle

The Cheerleader

The Cheerleader epitomizes school spirit, always front and center at every game and rally. Her energy and smiles are infectious, but her loyalty is selective. With a squad that follows her commands as closely as they follow her routines, she wields her popularity like a wand.

At Jefferson High, Friday nights are synonymous with football games and the frenzied cheers accompanying them. At the heart of this excitement stands Amanda, the Cheerleader whose high ponytail and flawless routines command the attention of everyone from students to the reluctant janitors. More than just a spirited girl in a uniform, Amanda is the queen of the field and the hallways, setting trends and standards across the school. Her charm is undeniable, her smiles as bright as the pep rally bonfires. However, her loyalty and kindness are selective and reserved for those who match her standards of popularity and spirit.

Ellie, always more comfortable with cameras than crowds, was inadvertently in Amanda's orbit during her first football game. She was there to take photos for the school's yearbook, not to socialize. Yet, she couldn't help but feel awed and alienated by Amanda's magnetic presence. The real challenge came weeks later, on a crowded Monday morning, when

Ellie, lost in thought, collided with Amanda, spilling her morning smoothie all over Amanda's pristine cheer uniform. The glare Amanda gave her was colder than the smoothie itself, and the whisper that followed Ellie around for weeks branded her as "clumsy" and "invisible"—a nobody who had messed up big time.

In the following days, Ellie spent much time contemplating the incident, feeling smaller with each whispered giggle and pointed stare. But as the days turned into weeks, she started to understand the dynamics of Amanda's influence, built on a foundation of visibility and validation from others—a fragile sort of power that Ellie realized she didn't need to covet. She took to the darkroom, pouring her frustrations and feelings into her photography. In the quiet red glow, she found beauty in shadows and strength in solitude. Her photos, particularly a candid shot of the mascot tripping over a cheerleader's pompom, won a school-wide contest, reminding her that recognition can come from unexpected places.

Instead of trying to fit into Amanda's circle, Ellie nurtured friendships with her fellow art club members and a couple of thoughtful bookworms from her English class. These people laughed at her jokes, appreciated her insights, and never made her feel small. During the homecoming game, as Amanda led a particularly vigorous cheer, she reached for her pom-poms. She grabbed the mascot's head instead, hoisting it high before realizing her mistake. The crowd erupted in laughter, and even Amanda couldn't help but join in. Ellie captured this moment, a rare break in Amanda's perfect facade, and it became a favorite in the yearbook.

By the end of the football season, Ellie had come to a powerful realization: Amanda's reign as the queen of the field didn't need to overshadow her existence. The real victory was embracing her uniqueness and finding esteem not in others' applause but in her quiet accomplishments.

Clara Belle

The Social Media Queen

This girl offers a modern twist on the mean girl archetype, leveraging digital platforms to influence and intimidate.

At Jefferson High, whispers and rumors once confined to hallways now ripple across screens with the speed of light, all thanks to the reigning social media Queen, Chloe. With her perfectly curated Instagram feed and a Snapchat story always buzzing with activity, Chloe sets the digital trends and, with them, the social standards of the school.

Ellie first encountered Chloe's digital domain during a school project that required students to follow each other's social media for a week. Chloe's posts blended glamorous selfies and exclusive party invites. They veiled jabs at those who didn't cut her weekend escapades. It wasn't long before Ellie was unwittingly tagged in a meme that poked fun at her quiet demeanor. This post quickly gathered likes and laughing emojis.

The digital snub stung, but it also sparked Ellie's realization about the ephemeral nature of online fame. Chloe's power, she understood, was as lasting as her latest post, constantly needing validation to sustain her queenly status. Ellie decided to use her social media as a tool not for popularity but for positivity. She started sharing her photography, capturing candid moments of school life that included the highs and the sincere, everyday interactions that often went unnoticed.

As Ellie's followers grew, so did her understanding of the influence she wielded. She learned to sympathize with Chloe, seeing her as a tormentor and as someone caught up in the relentless cycle of likes and shares. The turning point came when Ellie posted a series of photos from a school event, including a candid of Chloe helping a freshman fix her makeup—a rare glimpse of kindness that Chloe herself shared on her profile, captioned, "Sometimes, it's nice to be nice."

By the end of the year, Ellie had carved out her niche, creating a space where authenticity thrived over appearance. Her final post of the school year, a collage of her favorite shots, included a thank-you note to her followers for seeing the beauty in the genuine moments.

Clara Belle

She said that while the digital world is vast and varied, there is always room for kindness and real connections.

Clara Belle

The Intellectual Snob

The Intellectual Snob is a mean girl who uses her intellect as a weapon to assert dominance and belittle others; she allows others to explore a different kind of social challenge, one that revolves around academic and intellectual prowess.

In the quieter corners of Jefferson High's library, where the stacks cast long shadows, and the silence is almost tangible, resides Jenna, the Intellectual Snob. With her sharp wit and sharper tongue, she presides over study sessions and debate team meetings, wielding facts and philosophical quotes like dueling swords.

Ellie, though academically gifted, always dreaded interactions with Jenna. Her first real challenge came during a debate team tryout, where Jenna's critique of Ellie's argument was less constructive and more a public display of intellectual humiliation. The experience was painful but illuminated Jenna's true motive: insecurity masked by intellectual superiority.

Determined not to let Jenna's words define her intellect, Ellie began to seek knowledge for the joy of learning rather than to compete. She joined a science club where curiosity was encouraged, and mistakes were seen as steps to understanding, not failures. Here, Ellie found her confidence, not by knowing all the answers but by asking thoughtful questions and genuinely engaging with the material.

Ellie's new approach was noticed. Her science project on the biodiversity of the school's campus won her not only the school science fair but also respect from her peers and teachers for her thorough research and innovative presentation. Jenna, who was also in the competition, noticed Ellie's growing confidence and respect among the students.

The climax of their interaction came during a joint project where their teacher paired them together, hoping to bridge the gap between their talents. During their collaboration, Ellie's genuine enthusiasm and willingness to learn from everyone softened Jenna's need to always be the smartest in the room. They found common ground in their shared love for astronomy. Jenna's defenses began to lower as she realized that intellectual superiority didn't need to be lonely.

By the project's end, Jenna had learned to appreciate Ellie's different approach to learning, and Ellie had gained a new friend—or at least, a respected academic peer. Their final presentation was a success academically and a testament to their personal growth.

Clara Belle

The Gossip Guru

This mean girl thrives on the power of information and rumors.

At Jefferson High, where secrets are the currency of the corridors, no one trades more skillfully than Lila, the Gossip Guru. With a network that spans every clique and corner, Lila knows everything about everyone—and if she doesn't, she's adept at filling in the gaps with her creative assumptions.

Ellie first became aware of Lila's influence when a distorted story about her supposed rivalry with another student photographer spread through the school. The rumor, harmless at first, soon took on a life of its own, affecting Ellie's friendships and even her confidence in her photography.

Realizing the destructive power of unchecked gossip, Ellie tackled the issue at its source. She approached Lila directly, not with confrontation, but with a proposal: Ellie would provide authentic stories about the school's various clubs and activities for Lila's blog. In return, Lila would agree to verify her scoops before publishing them.

Surprisingly, Lila was receptive. The blog began to feature well-researched, exciting stories that celebrated student achievements and school events—more engaging material than the usual rumors. Ellie's initiative not only improved the blog's content but also subtly shifted Lila's role from a purveyor of gossip to a news reporter.

The transformation was not overnight; Lila occasionally slipped back into old habits. However, the positive feedback from the school community on the new blog direction encouraged her to stick to facts more often. Over time, Lila's blog became a respected source of school news, and Ellie helped foster a healthier communication culture at Jefferson High.

As the school year drew to a close, Ellie reflected on how she had turned a potential adversary into a collaborator, changing the narrative from division to unity and respect. She learned that sometimes the best way to combat misinformation is truth and transparency, and even the most notorious gossip can change her ways.

Clara Belle

The Fashionista

This mean girl dominates the school's fashion scene and uses her sense of style to create and enforce a social pecking order.

In the world of Jefferson High, where trends come and go with the seasons, Bianca, known as The Fashionista, dictates what's in and hopelessly out. With an eye for style and a knack for sharp critiques, she turns the school hallways into her runway, and her approval can elevate or sink the social stock of her classmates.

Ellie, whose wardrobe was more functional than fashionable, found herself unwittingly in Bianca's crosshairs during a school-wide assembly where Bianca made a snide remark about Ellie's worn-out sneakers. The comment was small, but the laughter it sparked was not, and Ellie felt a familiar flush of embarrassment.

But instead of shrinking back, Ellie saw an opportunity. She started a blog, "Function Over Fashion," where she showcased her style, one that prioritized comfort and individuality over high fashion. The blog featured interviews with students about their fashion choices, highlighting stories of self-expression and functionality—like a junior who modified his shoes to manage his foot braces better.

Bianca initially scoffed at Ellie's efforts, but as the blog gained popularity, she began to see the appeal in Ellie's celebration of personal style. The turning point came when Bianca stumbled upon a post about vintage thrift finds that included a piece remarkably similar to one she had recently flaunted as a high-end purchase. Intrigued and humbled, Bianca approached Ellie to feature a collaboration piece on vintage fashion.

The collaboration was a hit, blending Bianca's flair for high fashion with Ellie's eye for unique, sustainable choices. It broke new ground for both, with Bianca appreciating styles outside her usual luxury brands and Ellie recognizing the artistry in fashion design.

By the end of the school year, Bianca had transformed from a trend tyrant to a style savant who appreciated diversity in fashion. Ellie, on her part, had carved a niche for herself in the school's cultural tapestry, showing that style is not just what you wear but how you wear it—with confidence and authenticity.

Clara Belle

The Artistically Talented

This mean girl uses her creative skills to dominate and sometimes overshadow others in artistic spaces at school.

At Jefferson High, the art room is a sanctuary for the creatively inclined, where colors and concepts flourish. However, even this sanctuary has its guardian, Vanessa, known as The Artistically Talented. With undeniable skill and a portfolio of awards, Vanessa sets the standard for what is considered 'good art' at school. While often valid, her critiques can be sharp and dismissive, making her peers hesitant to showcase their work.

Ellie, who had always enjoyed photography as a hobby, was increasingly intimidated by Vanessa's presence in the art club. Her first real challenge came when Vanessa casually dismissed Ellie's photo exhibit idea for the school festival as "predictable and amateurish." The comment stung, and Ellie considered abandoning her project altogether.

But instead of retreating, Ellie embraced her artistic vision more fully. She dedicated herself to capturing the essence of everyday school life, focusing on the overlooked moments that made up the true spirit of

Jefferson High. She reached out to other students who felt overshadowed by Vanessa's dominance, encouraging them to contribute their work to her exhibit under the theme "Unseen Perspectives."

The exhibit became a collective effort, showcasing a range of artistic expressions from students who were previously reluctant to display their work. Vanessa, initially skeptical, was taken aback by the depth and diversity of the exhibit. Seeing the school through the lens of her peers, she began to appreciate the value of art forms that differed from her own.

The success of "Unseen Perspectives" not only boosted the confidence of many budding artists but also softened Vanessa's approach to her artistry. She started to offer more constructive feedback and became more open to collaboration, realizing that art could be a unifying force rather than a competitive arena.

By the end of the school year, the art club had transformed into a more inclusive and supportive community, with Vanessa and Ellie leading workshops together, each learning from the other's strengths. Ellie had found her place and helped redefine the artistic culture at Jefferson High, proving that every artist has a unique voice worthy of being heard.

Clara Belle

<u>The Undercover Mean Girl</u>

This character appears sweet and innocent but manipulates situations subtly and skillfully behind the scenes.

In the sprawling social landscape of Jefferson High, few students are as universally liked as Sarah, known for her sweet demeanor and seemingly genuine kindness. Yet beneath this veneer of innocence, Sarah operates as The Undercover Mean Girl, skillfully manipulating social situations to maintain her status without appearing overtly cruel.

With her keen observational skills, Ellie was one of the few who noticed the subtle shifts in Sarah's behavior: a whispered word here, a small action there, all seemingly innocuous but cumulatively powerful in shaping social dynamics. Ellie realized Sarah's true nature when she overheard Sarah subtly steering a teacher away from recognizing another student's achievements, suggesting instead that the accolades were undeserved.

Rather than confront Sarah directly—a move that would likely backfire given Sarah's mastery of her innocent image—Ellie decided to counteract Sarah's influence indirectly. She began a blog series titled

"Unsung Heroes" on the school's website, highlighting students' efforts and achievements that often went unnoticed. Each post was meticulously researched and verified, providing a platform for recognition that was harder for Sarah to manipulate.

As the blog gained traction, students and teachers started paying more attention to the diverse contributions of their peers, reducing the effectiveness of Sarah's behind-the-scenes maneuvering. Gradually, Sarah had to adapt to a school environment where her subtle tactics were less effective.

The turning point came when Ellie wrote a feature on a student who had quietly organized community service projects but had never sought recognition. The article led to the student receiving a community award, an outcome Sarah had tried to prevent earlier in the year. Seeing the positive impact of the recognition on the student's confidence, Sarah began to question the necessity of her manipulative tactics.

By the end of the year, Sarah's behavior had shifted noticeably. She became more openly supportive of her peers, finding that this approach bolstered her popularity in more genuine and fulfilling ways. Through her blog, Ellie highlighted the unsung heroes of Jefferson High and influenced a significant change in one of its most complicated characters.

Clara Belle

The New Girl

Ah…. The New Girl. She uses her novelty to disrupt existing social orders and strategically positions herself within the school's hierarchy.

At Jefferson High, the arrival of a new student is a common occurrence. Still, when Emily arrived mid-semester, she quickly became the center of attention. As The New Girl, Emily used her novelty and mysterious past to captivate the student body, swiftly climbing the social ladder by aligning herself with various influential groups.

Ellie watched with curiosity and caution as Emily navigated the social scene with surprising agility. Her charm and tales of her life in various cities worldwide drew people to her, and she skillfully played the role of the intriguing outsider. However, Ellie noticed that Emily's stories often shifted slightly depending on her audience. This tactic raised Ellie's suspicions about her sincerity.

Instead of challenging Emily directly, Ellie focused on strengthening the bonds within her circle of friends, emphasizing trust and genuine connections. She organized group activities that encouraged teamwork and shared experiences, like a photography project capturing the essence of their town through different lenses.

As these group activities became more popular, other students began to see the value in authentic relationships over the allure of novelty. Feeling her influence wane as students gravitated towards more genuine friendships, Emily realized she needed to adjust her approach.

The shift came during a school project where Emily was paired with Ellie. Forced to work together, Emily's facade began to crack, revealing insecurities about constantly moving and never having a stable group of friends. Understanding the underlying issues, Ellie helped Emily see that lasting relationships are built on honesty and reliability, not just on being the perpetual new girl with exciting stories.

Gradually, Emily began to open up more genuinely about her experiences, finding that her classmates appreciated her more for her realness than her mystique. By the end of the school year, Emily had formed true friendships based on more than just her novelty. Ellie's initiative to foster a culture of authenticity had transformed the social dynamics at Jefferson High.

Clara Belle

The Athlete

This mean girl uses her physical prowess and competitive spirit to dominate social interactions at school as well as in sports.

At Jefferson High, the sports fields are battlegrounds where physical prowess can translate into social power. This is the realm of Jessica, known as The Athlete, whose dominance in multiple sports has given her a near-celebrity status among her peers. With her competitive spirit and natural leadership skills, Jessica often blurs the lines between healthy competition and social intimidation.

Though not athletically inclined, Ellie found herself on Jessica's radar during the inter-class softball tournament. As the photographer for the school's sports teams, Ellie was used to capturing the highs and lows of sports events. However, during one intense game, Jessica's competitive nature took a harsh turn as she belittled teammates for their mistakes, including Ellie, who missed a shot that could have won her class the game.

Instead of shrinking under Jessica's harsh words, Ellie used the experience to fuel a new project: a photo essay on the true spirit of sportsmanship. She focused on moments of teamwork, encouragement, and mutual respect, contrasting these with the negative aspects of excessive competitiveness. The project was displayed in the school's main hallway and quickly sparked conversations about the values promoted in school sports.

Seeing her actions through Ellie's lens led Jessica to a moment of self-reflection. The praise for the photos that highlighted positive interactions and the critical discussions around the photos showing poor sportsmanship made her realize the impact of her behavior on her peers.

Motivated to change, Jessica started using her influence to foster a more supportive team environment. She began organizing post-game discussions where players could give each other constructive feedback and celebrate each other's efforts, regardless of the game's outcome.

By the end of the school year, Jessica had transformed from a feared competitor to a respected leader, admired for her athletic skills and dedication to promoting true sportsmanship. Ellie's project changed the sports culture at Jefferson High. It deepened her understanding of how leadership could be a force for good.

Clara Belle

The Sidekick

This mean girl doesn't lead but reinforces the actions of the queen bee, adding her twist of cruelty while staying under the radar.

In the social hierarchy of Jefferson High, while the queen bees grab the spotlight, their loyal sidekicks operate in the shadows. Among these, Mia stands out as The Sidekick, always seen but seldom heard, her influence subtle but significant. She amplifies the whims of her leader, Amanda, the Cheerleader from our earlier chapter, by spreading rumors, enforcing social exclusions, and often doing the dirty work that keeps their clique on top.

By now well-versed in the dynamics of mean girls, Ellie recognized Mia's role but also saw something else: a desire to be more than just a follower. During a group project, Ellie had the opportunity to work closely with Mia and noticed her often hesitating before echoing Amanda's harsh words as if conflicted.

Seizing the chance to understand Mia better, Ellie initiated a photography project focused on "Hidden Voices" at the school. She invited Mia to participate, allowing her to express her ideas and thoughts through photographs, separate from her identity as a sidekick.

As Mia engaged more with the project, she began to find her voice, showcasing her unique perspective on school life through her lens. Her photographs, distinct and thoughtful, gained recognition in their own right, encouraging her to step out from Amanda's shadow and engage with others more openly and authentically.

The project culminated in an exhibition, with Mia's work among the highlights, celebrated for its creativity and insight. The positive feedback bolstered her confidence, diminishing her reliance on her role as a sidekick for validation. Ellie's gentle guidance allowed Mia to redefine her identity at school.

By the end of the school year, Mia had transformed from a silent supporter of mean girl antics to an independent and respected student body member. Her journey from the background to a stand-alone figure demonstrated the power of finding and asserting one's voice to her peers.

Clara Belle

The Perfectionist

This mean girl imposes her high standards on herself and everyone around her—often leading to stress and unrealistic expectations.

At Jefferson High, perfection is personified in Grace, known among her peers as The Perfectionist. Her impeccable grades, flawless presentations, and meticulously planned school events set an awe-inspiring and unattainable standard for many. Her drive for perfection, while admirable, often manifests as criticism and impatience towards those who don't meet her high standards.

Ellie first felt the sting of Grace's perfectionism during a collaborative science project. Grace's relentless pursuit of flawlessness made the group work tense and stressful, overshadowing the joy of discovery with the fear of making mistakes.

Determined to address Grace's perfectionism's negative impact, Ellie proposed a new initiative for the school's annual science fair: a section dedicated to "Experimental Learning," where the focus would be on the process of exploration and learning from failures rather than just presenting perfect results. She encouraged

Grace to help organize this section, hoping it would show her the value of imperfect efforts.

While working together on the fair, Grace encountered various projects where errors led to unexpected breakthroughs and innovations. Interacting with enthusiastic students about their "failed" experiments and the lessons they learned, Grace began to see the beauty and importance of imperfection in the learning process.

The science fair was a success, particularly the "Experimental Learning" section, which became a highlight of the event. Grace's perspective shifted as she realized that her pursuit of perfection was stressful for herself and stifling for others. This revelation led her to ease her expectations for herself and her peers, fostering a more collaborative and supportive environment.

By the end of the school year, Grace had transformed from a rigid perfectionist into a more flexible and understanding leader. Her new approach improved her relationships and enhanced her learning as she embraced the unpredictability and creativity of accepting imperfection.

Clara Belle

The Lawyer's Daughter

We all know one of these. This mean girl uses her family's status and influence to assert dominance—and often gets her way academically *and* socially.

In the corridors of Jefferson High, Sophia, known as The Lawyer's Daughter, wields her family's influence like a gavel, often reminding her peers and even teachers of her powerful connections. Her confidence is bolstered by the belief that her actions have few real consequences, given her family's ability to navigate any trouble she might encounter.

Ellie, often on the quieter side of school politics, was directly impacted by Sophia's influence during the selection process for the school debate team. Despite Ellie's well-prepared audition, Sophia used her sway to secure a spot for her friend, leaving Ellie unfairly excluded.

Rather than confront Sophia directly, Ellie decided to channel her efforts into creating an alternative platform where every student could voice their opinions. She founded a school podcast called "Voices of Jefferson," which covered everything from school news to student editorials, providing a medium where equity in speech was valued over social standing.

As the podcast grew in popularity, Sophia began to notice its impact. Students who had never participated in debates were now sharing insightful commentaries and gaining a following. The podcast was leveling the playing field, diminishing the influence of Sophia's tactics.

Seeing the positive community response and realizing her diminished sway, Sophia approached Ellie with a proposal to feature on the podcast. Initially skeptical, Ellie agreed that the topic would focus on fairness and transparency in school activities.

The episode featuring Sophia turned out to be a pivotal moment for both. Sophia confronted the reality of her actions and their impact on her peers. Ellie drew a reflective side out of Sophia that few had seen, opening up a dialogue about the use of privilege and influence in school settings.

By the end of the school year, Sophia had started to use her influence more responsibly, advocating for fairer processes in school elections and club selections. Ellie's initiative had not only provided a platform for free expression. Still, it had also nudged a powerful peer towards a more equitable use of her influence.

Clara Belle

The Girl with a Dark Secret

This mean girl's harsh exterior shields her vulnerabilities and hidden aspects of her life, which she fears could tarnish her image if revealed.

In the social ecosystem of Jefferson High, few students are as enigmatic as Rachel, known among her peers as The Girl with a Dark Secret. On the surface, she is strict and often harsh, using her biting humor and standoffish demeanor to keep others at arm's length. Behind this façade lies a complex reality that she fiercely guards—a family struggling with issues that she believes would undermine her social standing if known.

Ellie, whose approach has always been one of empathy and curiosity, noticed the inconsistencies in Rachel's behavior—moments of unexpected kindness shrouded quickly by her usual coldness. Intrigued and concerned, Ellie sought to connect with Rachel without directly prying into her personal life.

The opportunity came through a photography project focused on "The Faces of Jefferson High," aiming to capture the unseen sides of students. Ellie invited Rachel to participate, allowing her to portray herself as she wished to be seen. To Ellie's surprise, Rachel agreed, intrigued by the idea of controlling her narrative.

During their sessions, Rachel chose to depict aspects of her life that were both strong and vulnerable. The project became a cathartic experience for her, allowing her to express her complexities safely and artistically. The portrayal was honest and resonant, showing her peers there was more to her than her tough exterior.

The exhibit was well-received, with Rachel's portraits being compelling. This public acknowledgment of her multifaceted personality allowed Rachel to engage more openly with her classmates, reducing her need to use meanness as a defense.

Ellie's project revealed Rachel's hidden depth and sparked conversations among the students about empathy and understanding. By the end of the school year, Rachel had started to let down her guard, finding that her true self, vulnerabilities and all, was accepted and even embraced by her peers.

Clara Belle

The Drama Diva

She lives for the spotlight and treats every school day like a Broadway debut. Her flair for the dramatic turns minor disagreements into soap opera-worthy confrontations. She's known for her signature eye roll and the dramatic toss of her meticulously styled hair.

At Jefferson High, drama class is more than just an elective—it's Cassandra's kingdom, where she reigns supreme, both on stage and off. With every day treated like a scene from a classic play, Cassandra's life is a series of dramatic entrances and exits, her emotions as embellished as her wardrobe.

For Cassandra, the drama room is a sanctuary where her rule is uncontested, and her flair for the theatrical is matched only by her need for constant attention. Whether it's reciting Shakespearean monologues between classes or turning a minor disagreement into a tearful tragedy, Cassandra ensures all eyes are on her.

Ellie, known for her quiet demeanor and observational skills, initially found Cassandra's dramatics amusing until her own life became part of Cassandra's script. When Ellie accidentally spills water near Cassandra's freshly painted scenery, Cassandra unleashes a soliloquy about betrayal and ruin that could rival the Bard himself. The incident, minor to Ellie, was transformed into a saga of epic proportions, with Cassandra as the tragic heroine, wronged by fate and a clumsy classmate.

Rather than shrink under the weight of Cassandra's dramatized wrath, Ellie decided to use her photography project to showcase a different narrative. She titled it "Behind the Curtains," capturing candid moments of various drama club members, including Cassandra, in their on-stage bravado and off-stage vulnerability.

Ellie's project revealed the often-unseen aspects of the drama club: the teamwork, the nervous preparations, and the genuine joy of performance. Her photographs of Cassandra showed a side rarely seen by the school—a dedicated actress who cared deeply for her craft beyond just the applause.

The exhibit was an eye-opener for many, including Cassandra, who saw her theatrical persona captured in a humanizing light. The positive feedback from her peers, who appreciated seeing the real effort behind the dramatic façade, made Cassandra realize the power of authenticity over constant performance.

Gradually, Cassandra began to tone down her everyday theatrics, finding that her genuine interactions were as impactful as her staged ones. She started using her dramatic flair to uplift others in the drama club, helping them find their voices on the stage.

By the end of the school year, Cassandra had evolved from the uncontested queen of drama to a mentor and leader, appreciated not just for her theatrical talents but for her ability to inspire and support her fellow students.

Clara Belle

The Eco-Warrior

This girl is fiercely passionate about the environment—so much so that she judges everyone's recycling habits. She patrols the lunchroom to lecture on the virtues of composting and the evils of plastic straws, often making her classmates feel like they're one disposable cup away from ecological disaster.

At Jefferson High, Miranda is not just another student; she's the self-proclaimed guardian of the planet. As the president of the Environmental Club, she takes her role to heart, transforming every corner of the school into a battleground for ecological righteousness. Her commitment to sustainability is commendable as it is comical, often leading to extreme measures to ensure the school's carbon footprint is as minimal as possible.

From patrolling the cafeteria to ensure everyone sorts their waste correctly to lecturing unsuspecting first-year students about the dangers of single-use plastics, Miranda's methods are as forceful as well-intentioned. Her latest campaign? Banning all plastic utensils from the school premises—a move that led to an amusing week of students attempting to eat yogurt and soup with wooden chopsticks.

Ellie, always on the lookout for intriguing subjects, sees the humor and sincerity in Miranda's fervor. Deciding to document

Miranda's eco-campaigns, she begins a photo series titled "Green at School." The series captures Miranda in action—chasing down plastic bag offenders or watering the school garden at dawn—and highlights the quirky side of being eco-conscious at school.

One particularly memorable incident involves Miranda organizing a "flash mob" for composting awareness, where students suddenly freeze in the lunchroom holding up compostable items. The bewildered expressions of the uninitiated make for a series of humorous yet thought-provoking photographs that quickly go viral within the school community.

As the photo series gains popularity, students engage more actively with Miranda's initiatives, albeit with a smile. They start to see the fun in being eco-friendly, and Miranda's once stern lectures turn into interactive and enjoyable discussions. Her approach softens as she realizes that combining humor with activism is often more effective than stern admonishments.

The climax of Ellie's series is a shot of Miranda dressed as a giant recyclable bottle leading the Earth Day parade. This sight earns her the affectionate nickname "Eco-Warrior Queen" among her peers. This event marks a turning point in how students perceive environmental activism and helps Miranda see the value of including others in her mission with a lighter touch.

By the end of the school year, Miranda has transformed from a solitary eco-police officer to a beloved leader of a growing environmental movement at school. Her ability to laugh at herself and engage her peers with humor and creativity has broadened the reach of her campaigns and made her a more effective and admired leader.

The Tech Tyrant

This mean girl rules the school's tech lab with an iron fist. Suppose you need help with a computer issue. In that case, she's your girl—but be warned, for she will give you a condescending tutorial on why you should never have encountered this problem in the first place.

In the buzzing world of Jefferson High's tech lab, Emily reigns supreme. Known affectionately (and somewhat fearfully) as the Tech Tyrant, she is the undisputed master of all things digital. From debugging code to managing the school's online forums, Emily wields her tech prowess like a scepter, often accompanied by a smirk and a sassy comment about the digital illiteracy of her peers.

Her kingdom is the computer lab, where she presides over rows of screens and a legion of lesser techies. But her rule isn't just about power—it's about perfection. Every pixel must be in place, and every line of code must be pristine. This quest for digital perfection often leads to hilariously harsh critiques of her classmates' PowerPoint presentations, which she deems unworthy of the school's high-tech projectors.

Ever the observer, Ellie sees a story behind Emily's tyrannical facade. She decides to document a week in the life of the Tech Tyrant for the school newspaper, capturing both her iron-fisted rule and her unexpected acts of kindness—like the time she secretly helped a struggling student create a killer graphics project late into the night.

The highlight of Ellie's piece is an amusing incident during the school's "Tech-Free Day," which Emily protested by communicating exclusively through hand-written binary code. Her classmates' bafflement turned into amusement as they tried to decode her messages, only to find them to be witty remarks about the archaic nature of pen and paper.

As the week progresses, Ellie's photographs and articles reveal more than just the tyrant in Emily. They show a passionate, albeit prickly, genius who genuinely wants to elevate everyone's tech skills, not just showcase her own; her tricky exterior cracks when she sees how her peers respond positively to her less authoritarian, more teacher-like approach.

Inspired by the positive feedback, Emily starts a weekly tech clinic, humorously dubbed "Tyranny Tutoring," where she offers her expertise in a more friendly and approachable manner. The sessions are a hit, blending Emily's sharp wit with genuinely helpful tech tips, making technology more accessible and less intimidating for everyone.

By the end of the school year, Emily's transformation from tyrant to teacher is complete. Her new role as a mentor has made the tech lab a more welcoming place and softened her image, turning the Tech Tyrant into the Tech Titan, a leader who empowers rather than intimidates.

Clara Belle

The PTA Princess

She wields power through her mom's heavy involvement in the Parent-Teacher Association (PTA). She knows about policy changes and teacher gossip before anyone else, and she isn't afraid to use this information to her advantage.

At Jefferson High, Julie holds a unique position of influence, not through her achievements but through her mother's prominent role in the Parent-Teacher Association. Dubbed the PTA Princess, Julie's insights into school policy changes and administrative gossip are unmatched. Her knowledge makes her a valuable ally or a daunting adversary, depending on which side of the school policy you find yourself.

Julie's reign is marked by her ability to sway school decisions, from dress codes to fundraiser themes, often tipping the scales in favor of her social circle. Her signature move is dropping veiled hints about upcoming changes, and she watches with amusement as her classmates scramble to align with the new rules.

Ellie finds Julie's blend of power and pettiness fascinating and decides to feature her in the school newsletter. The article aims to uncover how Julie uses her information for influence and whether her reign could be swayed towards more benevolent governance.

A particularly humorous yet eye-opening event occurs during the annual school spirit week. With insider knowledge, Julie pushes for a 1980s retro theme, knowing well that her wardrobe is stocked with perfect outfits. Her classmates, however, scramble to thrift shops and parents' closets, resulting in a hilariously mismatched array of styles that more closely resembles a time-travel mishap than a decade tribute.

Ellie captures this chaos in a photo series, juxtaposing Julie's polished Madonna-esque ensemble with the less accurate but more spirited attempts of her peers. The photos, accompanied by light-hearted commentary, become a hit among the student body, revealing the absurdity and fun of the situation.

Seeing the positive response to the newsletter feature, Julie begins to realize the power of her position could be used to unite rather than divide. Inspired by the spirit week's unexpected success in bringing students together, Julie starts to channel her insider knowledge into creating events that cater to a broader variety of interests, not just her own.

She collaborates with Ellie on a project to make PTA meetings more transparent and student-friendly, initiating a series of "PTA Declassified" sessions where students can voice their concerns and suggestions directly. These sessions help demystify the PTA's workings and turn Julie from a gatekeeper of secrets into a bridge between students and school administration.

By the end of the school year, Julie's transformation from a princess guarding her castle of secrets to a leader fostering community involvement redefines her role at Jefferson High. She learns that influence comes not from wielding power over others but from empowering them.

Clara Belle

The Snack Shack Queen

This mean girl controls the most trafficked area in school—the snack shack. Her approval can get you the freshest bagels or leave you with the stale donuts.

In the bustling hub of Jefferson High, the snack shack serves as the epicenter of midday munching—and Natasha, dubbed the Snack Shack Queen, rules over this kingdom of confections with a sweet but iron fist. Her reign is characterized by her control over the snack inventory, deciding who gets the freshest bagels and who must contend with the day-old donuts.

Natasha's rule isn't just about snack distribution; it's a complex web of trade and favors. Need a prime spot in line during a big game day? That'll cost you two homework answers or a favor to be named later. Her currency is snacks, and business is booming.

Ellie, always keen to explore the unique cultures within her school, sees a ripe opportunity for a humorous exposé in the school newspaper. She goes undercover to document a week in the life of the Snack Shack Queen, detailing the bartering, the backdoor deals, and the bizarre economy that Natasha has created.

One particularly amusing incident involves Natasha orchestrating a covert exchange of cinnamon rolls for a coveted copy of the upcoming math test. Ellie captures this moment through candid photos, showcasing Natasha's knack for snack-based diplomacy.

As the article takes shape, Natasha's realm of influence is humorously revealed, as are her cleverness and business acumen. Students begin to see the snack shack not just as a place for quick bites but as a microcosm of supply and demand, with Natasha as its savvy overseer.

Seeing herself portrayed with a mix of humor and respect in Ellie's piece, Natasha begins to appreciate her role from a new perspective. She started implementing a "Snack Shack Points" system, where students can earn snacks through positive contributions to the school community, such as tutoring peers or participating in clean-up days.

This new system transforms the snack shack from a hub of petty deals into a force for good, encouraging student involvement and rewarding positive behavior. Natasha's image shifts from a cunning snack lord to a community leader, promoting a healthier, more inclusive atmosphere at the snack shack.

By the end of the school year, Natasha's evolution from a snack baron to a community benefactor changes the dynamics of midday trading. This enriches the school culture and proves that even the most unlikely places can foster community and cooperation.

Clara Belle

The Hallway Monitor

Who can forget this mean girl? She is self-appointed and takes her unofficial position a little too seriously. She's known for handing out "citations" for running in the halls and laughing excessively loudly.

At Jefferson High, the hallways are more than just passageways between classes—they are Hannah's domain. Dubbed the Hallway Monitor, although unofficially so, Hannah takes it upon herself to enforce a peculiar set of rules, from the proper walking speed to the acceptable conversation volume. Armed with a whistle, she bought herself a clipboard full of self-made citations. She patrolled the corridors with an earnestness that borders on the comical.

Hannah's dedication to maintaining order is both admired and mocked. Her strict "no running" policy is infamous, and she's been known to give detailed lectures on the hazards of hurried movement, complete with hand-drawn diagrams and statistics from dubious sources.

Ellie finds both humor and a hint of tyranny in Hannah's self-appointed role and decides to feature her in a light-hearted documentary for the school's digital media class. The project aims to explore the quirky side of

Hannah's rule, capturing both the absurdity and the unexpected benefits of her vigilant monitoring.

One of the funniest segments involves Hannah implementing a "hallway lane system," where she attempts to direct traffic by taping lanes onto the floor, designating them for walkers, runners, and dawdlers. The result is a confused mix of students trying to adhere to the lanes, leading to a humorous but chaotic traffic pattern that Ellie captures brilliantly in her film.

As the documentary circulates, students and faculty begin to see Hannah in a new light. While her methods are unorthodox and often overly strict, they stem from a genuine desire to keep everyone safe and organized. Her commitment and creativity in pursuing this goal earned her a mixture of respect and affection from the school community.

Realizing the impact of her documentary, Ellie encourages Hannah to channel her passion for order into more productive and less intrusive initiatives. Together, they work to create a student-led safety committee, giving Hannah a legitimate platform to contribute to school safety without overstepping her bounds.

The safety committee became a success, allowing Hannah to apply her rules in a way that involved the community and received official backing. Her transition from a lone enforcer to a respected leader in the safety committee changes her from a figure of ridicule to one of respect.

By the end of the school year, Hannah has learned to balance her love for order with the freedom of her peers, turning her hallway monitoring into a collaborative effort that promotes safety and respect across the school.

Clara Belle

The Book Club Boss

This mean girl not only decides the reading list but critiques anyone who dares to interpret the symbolism of "The Great Gatsby" differently than she does.

In the quiet corners of Jefferson High's library, where the whispers of pages turning should be the loudest sound, Vanessa, known as the Book Club Boss, rules with an iron bookmark. Her command over the monthly reading selections is absolute, and she enforces her interpretations of literary works with the zeal of a seasoned critic. Disagreeing with Vanessa on the themes of "The Great Gatsby"? Prepare for a well-rehearsed monologue about the green light and the American Dream.

While effective in maintaining order in the book club discussions, Vanessa's leadership style often stifles creativity and individual expression. Her book club meetings are less discussions and more lectures, with Vanessa at the podium delivering her verdicts on character motivations and symbolic meanings.

Ellie, an occasional book club attendee, sees both the humor and the tyranny in Vanessa's rule. Inspired, she decides to start a blog series, "Alternative Book Club," which explores different interpretations of the same books discussed in Vanessa's meetings. Each blog post invites guest students to share their views, providing a democratic contrast to Vanessa's autocratic book club.

One particularly amusing blog post reinterprets "Lord of the Flies" as a misunderstood comedy, complete with absurd evidence and tongue-in-cheek analysis. The post goes viral within the school, sparking laughs and lively debate among students and faculty alike.

As the blog gains popularity, Vanessa finds her authority challenged. Surprisingly, instead of clamping down, she shows up at one of the "Alternative Book Club" discussions. Expecting confrontation, the group is stunned when Vanessa engages with the alternative interpretations with genuine interest and humor.

This shift marks a turning point for Vanessa. She begins to loosen her grip on the book club, incorporating more open discussions and featuring guest speakers from Ellie's blog. The book club transforms from a dictatorship into a vibrant community of literary enthusiasts who appreciate diverse perspectives.

By the end of the school year, Vanessa has evolved from a dictator of the written word to a curator of a dynamic literary community. Her acceptance of multiple interpretations enriches the club's discussions, making it a favorite extracurricular activity among students. Vanessa learns that literature, like life, thrives on diversity and dialogue, not dogma.

Clara Belle

The Sarcasm Slinger

Everyone knows one of these; she has a biting wit that can leave her classmates laughing *and* crying. Her tongue is sharper than the pencils she never lends out.

Lucy, affectionately and fearfully dubbed the Sarcasm Slinger by her peers at Jefferson High, wields her wit like a sword, always ready to deliver a cutting remark with a smile. Her tongue is sharper than the pencils she refuses to lend, and her sarcasm serves as her armor and weapon.

Her reign of sarcastic terror includes commentary on everything from school lunches ("Ah yes, mystery meat Tuesday, a culinary guessing game.") to pep rallies ("Another pep rally? My enthusiasm knows no bounds."). While her barbs are often hilarious, they can sometimes sting too much, leaving her more feared than loved.

Ellie, always keen on capturing the essence of her classmates, sees an opportunity to showcase the intelligence behind Lucy's sarcasm. She proposes a collaboration for the school newspaper—a weekly column called "Lucy's Lookout," where Lucy can channel her sarcasm into humorous commentary on school events and social quirks.

One of the column's most popular entries features a sarcastic review of the school's attempt at a Shakespeare play, where Lucy suggests that the real tragedy was not the plot but the costumes. Her humorous take is both a critique and a celebration of the school's spirit, and it's received with laughter and appreciation, showing a side of Lucy that pokes fun without malice.

As the column gains popularity, Lucy begins to appreciate the power of her words to entertain and enlighten rather than just cut down. Her classmates start to see the cleverness in her sarcasm, not just the sharpness. This shift encourages Lucy to moderate her daily interactions, using her sarcasm to highlight absurdities and injustices in a way that provokes thought rather than just laughter or hurt.

Ellie's photographs of Lucy in action—capturing her mid-eye-roll or smirking behind a book—accompany the columns, providing a visual punchline to Lucy's verbal jabs. These images help humanize Lucy, showing her as a thinker and a humorist rather than just a cynic.

By the end of the school year, Lucy has transformed from a feared verbal duelist to a beloved satirist. Her column becomes a much-anticipated feature in the school newspaper, and she finds herself more integrated into the school's social fabric. She is respected for her sharp mind and is now appreciated for her heart.

Clara Belle

The Matchmaker Manipulator

Stay away from this mean girl. She fancies herself a Cupid, using her social clout to set up relationships and break them when she sees fit, all under the guise of "just trying to help."

Emma, known around Jefferson High as the Matchmaker Manipulator, wields her social clout to play Cupid, orchestrating romances and breakups with the precision of a chess master. She sees relationships not as matters of the heart but as social experiments, often under the guise of "just trying to help."

Her matchmaking schemes blend genuine insight into people's personalities and a mischievous enjoyment of the drama they create. Whether pairing the star quarterback with the quiet bookworm for a dance or breaking up a seemingly perfect couple due to a misinterpreted text message, Emma's interventions are always a hot topic.

Guided by the complexity of Emma's role and the effects of her meddling, Ellie decides to document her matchmaking adventures in a light-hearted investigative piece for the school's digital magazine. She follows Emma's maneuvers, interviewing her "victims" and charting the unforeseen consequences of her setups.

One particularly humorous incident involves Emma organizing a blind date event and mixing up the meeting places. A goth meets a star athlete at a poetry reading, and a tech geek shows up at a cheerleading practice. The mix-ups, while initially awkward, lead to unexpected friendships and some eye-opening conversations.

As Ellie publishes these stories, they spark laughter and provide a more profound reflection among students about the nature of relationships and the value of genuine connections. Emma reads the comments and feedback and begins to see the impact of her meddling in a new light.

Challenged by Ellie's articles to reconsider her approach, Emma uses her skills for good. She transforms her matchmaking into a "relationship workshop" where she helps people understand more about communication and compatibility rather than directly manipulating their romantic lives.

This shift turns Emma from a manipulative matchmaker into a respected relationship guru at the school. Her workshops are filled with laughter and learning, fostering a more sincere understanding of student relationships.

Emma has redefined her legacy at Jefferson High by the end of the school year. Her new role as a mentor in matters of the heart has earned her admiration and respect, proving that even the most mischievous inclinations can be channeled into positive community contributions.

Clara Belle

The Study Group Czar

She organizes all the major study groups and decides who gets in based on a quiz about how much you can contribute to the group's success.

At Jefferson High, Rachel holds the unofficial title of Study Group Czar. With her comprehensive knowledge and razor-sharp focus, she presides over study sessions with an iron will, deciding who can join based on their academic prowess and perceived dedication. Her study groups are infamous—highly effective but equally intimidating.

Rachel's leadership style involves rigorous quizzes to accompany her study sessions, turning preparation into a high-stress audition. Academically speaking, she believes in survival of the fittest, and her sessions reflect this with a competitive edge that often leaves less confident students in the dust.

Ellie, always interested in the dynamics of student interactions, sees an opportunity to soften Rachel's harsh reputation while showcasing the benefits of diverse study groups. She proposes a feature article for the school paper that will include a week-long documentary of Rachel's study groups, aiming to capture their intense yet effective nature.

One particularly amusing segment involves Rachel attempting to enforce a "whisper-only" rule in the library, leading to a series of comical misunderstandings and silent but dramatic gestures among the group members. The humor and absurdity of the situation, captured in Ellie's photos, bring a light-heartedness to Rachel's usually stern sessions.

As the article and photos circulate, they stir up discussions about the inclusivity of academic support at Jefferson High. Students start to voice their opinions, suggesting that study groups should be more welcoming and supportive rather than exclusive and stressful.

Taking these criticisms to heart, Rachel begins to rethink her approach. She starts to include collaborative games and group discussions in her sessions, making them more engaging and less competitive. She also opens her study groups to all students, regardless of their initial academic standing, focusing on mutual improvement rather than gatekeeping knowledge.

This transformation changes the atmosphere of her study sessions. It reshapes Rachel's image from a tyrannical tutor to a collaborative coach. Her groups grow in popularity, becoming a model for other study sessions around the school.

By the end of the school year, Rachel's study groups are no longer just a means to boost grades but a community effort that fosters learning and camaraderie among students. Rachel herself learns the value of leadership that empowers and unites rather than excludes and intimidates.

Clara Belle

Lessons from the School of Hard Knocks

Queen Bees and Wannabees: Outsmarting the School's Royalty

As the school year at Jefferson High draws to a close, the lessons learned extend far beyond the confines of textbooks and classroom lectures. The stories of our diverse characters—from Cassandra, the Drama Diva, to Grace, the Mistress of Precision—reveal the transformative power of empathy, humor, and self-reflection.

Ellie's journey through the school year, documenting the lives of these unique individuals, has not only provided her with rich material for her photography and articles but has also taught her and her peers invaluable life lessons. Each chapter of this book has offered a window into the challenges and changes that come with understanding and adapting to different personalities.

From Misunderstanding to Empathy:

Each profile has shown that beneath every harsh exterior or quirky habit lies a deeper story. By exploring these stories, Ellie and her classmates have learned to replace judgment with empathy, seeing their peers not just as 'mean girls' or 'tyrants' but as complex individuals with their fears, desires, and potential for growth.

The Power of Humor:

Humor has played a pivotal role in bridging gaps between students. By laughing together at the absurdities of high school life, the students of Jefferson High have found common ground, eased tensions, and fostered a more inclusive school environment.

Self-Reflection and Growth:

Each character's evolution throughout the book highlights the importance of self-reflection. As each witness and participate in each other's stories, students at Jefferson High learn to reflect on their actions and attitudes, leading to personal growth and change.

As Ellie compiles her final article for the school newspaper, she reflects on the impact of her work. Once just assignments, the profiles have become part of the school's culture, prompting discussions about identity, change, and community. The yearbook, filled with her photographs, is a testament to a year of unexpected lessons and friendships.

Looking Ahead:

As graduation approaches, Jefferson High students differ from those who started the year. They've grown wiser, kinder, and more understanding. The school has transformed, becoming a place where diversity in personality and thought is celebrated rather than feared.

Ellie closes her final article with a quote that has guided her through her project: "Everyone you meet is fighting a battle you know nothing about. Be kind. Always." With this, she challenges future classes to continue exploring and understanding the unique stories that each student brings to the halls of Jefferson High and the personal challenges that will influence their behavior and growth in the new school year.

Clara Belle

Queen Bees and Wannabees: Outsmarting the School's Royalty

Clara Belle

Queen Bees and Wannabees: Outsmarting the School's Royalty